C

love

r t Grandpa

X X

May 1993

A Treasury of Stories, Songs, and Poems About Bears

BEARS · BEARS · BEARS

Compiled by Mary Pope Osborne
Illustrated by Karen Lee Schmidt

SIMON & SCHUSTER BOOKS FOR YOUNG READERS
Published by Simon & Schuster
New York • London • Toronto • Sydney • Tokyo • Singapore

SIMON & SCHUSTER BOOKS FOR YOUNG READERS
Simon & Schuster Building, Rockefeller Center
1230 Avenue of the Americas, New York, New York 10020
Text copyright © 1990 by Parachute Press, Inc.
"Snow White and Rose Red" copyright © 1990 by Mary Pope Osborne.
Illustrations copyright © 1990 by Karen Lee Schmidt.
SIMON & SCHUSTER BOOKS FOR YOUNG READERS
is a trademark of Simon & Schuster.
Designed by Michel Design.
Manufactured in the United States of America.

10 9 8 7 6 5 4 3 2

Library of Congress Cataloging-in-Publication Data

Bears, bears, bears : a treasury of stories, songs, and poems about
   bears / compiled by Mary Pope Osborne : illustrated by Karen Lee
   Schmidt.
        p.   cm.
      Originally published: Englewood Cliffs, NJ : Silver Press, © 1990.
      Summary: Folklore, original stories, and poems about bears.
      1. Bears—Literary collections. [1. Bears—Literary
collections.] I. Osborne. Mary Pope. II. Schmidt, Karen. ill.
[PZ5.B38   1992]
808.8′036—dc20   92-12950
ISBN: 0-671-69631-9   CIP

ACKNOWLEDGMENTS

Every effort has been made to trace the ownership of all copyrighted material and to secure the necessary permissions to reprint these selections. If any question arises as to the use of any material, the editor and the publisher, while expressing regret for any inadvertent error, will make the necessary correction in future printings.

Grateful acknowledgment is made to the following for permission to reprint copyrighted material:

Atheneum Publishers, an imprint of Macmillan Publishing Co., for THE BEAR ON THE MOTORCYCLE by Reiner Zimnik, translated from the German by Cornelius Schaeffer, copyright © 1963 by Atheneum House, Inc.; Lois Lenski Covey Foundation for "The Bear" from CITY POEMS by Lois Lenski; Curtis Brown Ltd. for "Grandpa Bear's Lullaby" from DRAGON NIGHT AND OTHER LULLABIES by Jane Yolen, copyright © 1981 by Jane Yolen; Dutton Children's Books, a division of Penguin USA, for "Furry Bear" from NOW WE ARE SIX by A.A. Milne, copyright © 1927 by E.P. Dutton, renewed 1955 by A.A. Milne; and "In Which We Are Introduced to Winnie-the-Pooh and Some Bees, and the Stories Begin" from WINNIE-THE-POOH by A.A. Milne, illustrated by Ernest H. Shepard, copyright © 1926 by E.P. Dutton, renewed 1954 by A.A. Milne; Harcourt Brace Jovanovich, Inc. for "The Bear Hunt" from LITTLE GIRL AND BOY LAND by Margaret Widdemer, copyright © 1924 by Harcourt Brace Jovanovich, Inc., renewed 1952 by Margaret Widdemer Schauffler; Harper & Row for "The Bear and the Butterfly" from NIBBLE, NIBBLE by Margaret Wise Brown, text copyright © 1959 by William R. Scott, Inc., "The Bear and the Crow" from FABLES, written and illustrated by Arnold Lobel, copyright © 1980 by Arnold Lobel, and "Little Bear's Mermaid" from FATHER BEAR COMES HOME by Else Homelund Minarik, illustrated by Maurice Sendak, text copyright © 1959 by Else Homelund Minarik, illustrations copyright © 1959 by Maurice Sendak; Margaret Hillert for "Bear Cub's Day"; MacDonald H. Leach for "Kunikdjuaq: A Bear Story of the Inuit" from THE RAINBOW BOOK OF AMERICAN FOLK TALES AND LEGENDS by Maria Leach, copyright © 1958 by Maria Leach, renewed by MacDonald Leach; Macmillan of Canada, a division of Canada Publishing Corp., for "Good Night, Good Night" by Dennis Lee from JELLY BELLY by Dennis Lee; Gail Kredenser Mack for "Polar Bear" from THE ABC OF BUMPTIOUS BEASTS; Little, Brown & Co. for "Adventures of Isabel" from BAD PARENTS' GARDEN OF VERSES by Ogden Nash, copyright © 1936 by Ogden Nash; McClelland & Stewart for Canadian rights to "Furry Bear" from NOW WE ARE SIX by A.A. Milne, and "In Which We Are Introduced to Winnie-the-Pooh and Some Bees, and the Stories Begin" from WINNIE-THE-POOH by A.A. Milne, illustrated by Ernest Shepard; Peters Fraser & Dunlop Group Ltd. for "The Polar Bear" from THE BAD CHILD'S BOOK OF BEASTS by Hilaire Belloc; Scholastic, Inc. for THE FORGETFUL BEARS by Lawrence Weinberg, text copyright © 1981 by Lawrence Weinberg; Mary Chute Smith for "My Teddy Bear" from RHYMES ABOUT US by Marchette Chute, copyright © 1974 by E.P. Dutton, Inc.; Warner/Chappell Music, Inc. for "TEDDY BEAR PICNIC" by John W. Bratton and Jimmy Kennedy, copyright © 1907, renewed 1947 by Warner Bros., Inc.

Contents

To the Reader

I have always loved bears. When I was a child, I helped my younger brother, Michael, take care of a whole collection of teddy bear companions. My brother even went so far as to form his bears into a baseball team! After one game on a summer's day, we bathed a dusty player. He was never the same again. The bear's eyes fell out, and his coat became stiff and coarse. After that, we called him Poor Bear, although he made enough of a comeback to keep playing on the team.

The baseball captain was a giant teddy named Bosco. One summer Bosco and his teddy bear team played an entire World Series against my brother's rolled-up socks.

Today the word "bear" is my favorite term of endearment; I sometimes call my small terrier "Bear," I call the neighbors' golden retriever "Bear," I call my husband "Bear."

Why do bears inspire such affection and invention? I think because in no other animal is there a happier combination of cuddliness and wildness. The tender side of bears was mythologized in 1902 when news reporters spread the story that on a hunting trip to Mississippi, President Teddy Roosevelt had spared the life of a helpless bear cub. A popular cartoonist of the day, Clifford Berryman, drew a cartoon of that young bear with the President, and soon a Brooklyn toy maker began manufacturing soft, safe versions of "Teddy's Bear."

The creatures in this book run the gamut of bears—from quiet little teddy bears to enormous grizzlies. There are growly bears, forgetful bears, fuzzy wuzzy bears, bears who dream in cold winter caves, and bears who sleep in big, warm beds.

This collection represents a great variety of literary sources. A number of different cultures of the world are represented. There is an Alaskan tale, an African-American tale, and a Native American legend. There are bear tales first told at very different times in history—Aesop's bear is more than two thousand years old, and there are Norse and German stories from the Middle Ages.

There are read-aloud pieces for every occasion: soothing songs and nursery rhymes to lure children to sleep, silly poems and fables to make them laugh, picture-book adventures to thrill and excite them. Listeners will take part in a teddy bears' picnic and a circus bear's performance. They'll reunite with such familiar friends as the one curious bear who went over the mountain, the two bears named Pooh and Little Bear, and the three who are destined to meet a girl named Goldilocks. Brought to life again with the help of Karen Lee Schmidt's beautiful illustrations, these excellent bears will live on in our imaginations and help empower and protect each listening child.

We all need bears. In a world that is growing further and further away from nature, we need the bears of our dreams and stories to remind us of that which is ferocious yet tender, uncouth yet elegant, wild yet familiar. Who wouldn't love to trade places with Snow White and Rose Red as they play with their big wooly bear in front of the fire on a snowy night? I would. And I still long to be the child who runs away with the organ grinder's dancing bear:

> Oh, I looked at him and he winked at me,
> And my heart was light and the day was fair,
> And away I went with the dancing bear.

Mary Pope Osborne

B was once a little Bear,
Beary!
Wary!
Hairy!
Beary!
Taky cary!
Little Bear!

Edward Lear

There was an Old Person of Ware,
Who rode on the back of a Bear;
When they ask'd, "Does it trot?"
He said, "Certainly not!
He's a Moppsikon Floppsikon Bear!"

Edward Lear

Fuzzy Wuzzy was a bear;
Fuzzy Wuzzy had no hair.
Fuzzy Wuzzy wasn't fuzzy,
Was he?

Traditional

Polar Bear

The secret of the polar bear
Is that he wears long underwear.

Gail Kredenser

The Polar Bear

The Polar Bear is unaware
    Of cold that cuts me through:
For why? He has a coat of hair.
    I wish I had one too!

Hilaire Belloc

Teddy Bear, Teddy Bear

Teddy Bear, Teddy Bear,
Go upstairs.

Teddy Bear, Teddy Bear,
Say your prayers.

Teddy Bear, Teddy Bear,
Turn out the light.

Teddy Bear, Teddy Bear,
Say good night.

Round and Round
the Garden

Round and round the garden,
Like a teddy bear;

One step,
Two step,

Tickly under there!

The Story of the Three Bears

nursery tale and rebus

Once upon a time, three bears lived in a 🏠 in the woods. When they cooked porridge for their breakfast one morning, the bears found that it was too hot to eat. While the porridge cooled, they went for a walk in the 🌲🌲🌲 .

While the bears were gone, a girl walked by their 🏠 . Her name was Goldilocks, and she had been out in the 🌲🌲🌲 chasing a 🦋 . When she came to the 🏠 of the 🐻🐻🐻 , she peeked in the window and saw that nobody was home. When 👧 tried the front 🚪 , she found that it wasn't locked. So she walked right in.

On the kitchen 🪑 , Goldilocks saw three bowls of porridge. When she tasted the porridge in Papa Bear's 🥣 , she found it was too hot. When she tasted the porridge in Mama Bear's 🥣 , she found it was too cold. When she tasted the porridge in Baby Bear's 🥣 , she found it was just right. So she ate it all up.

Then 👧 saw three chairs. When she sat in Papa Bear's 🪑 , she found it was too hard. When she sat in Mama Bear's 🛋️ , she found it was too soft. When she saw Baby Bear's 🪑 , it looked just right. But when she sat down, the bottom of the 🪑 fell out!

Next 🐑 climbed up the 🪜 . In the bedroom she found three beds. When she lay down on Papa Bear's 🛏 , she found it was too hard. When she lay down on Mama Bear's 🛏 , she found it was too soft. When she lay down on Baby Bear's 🛏 , it felt just right. So 🐑 closed her 👀 and went to sleep.

While 🐑 slept, the 🐻 returned from their walk in the 🌲 .

When Papa Bear sat down at the kitchen table, he saw a 🥄 in his 🥣 . "SOMEBODY HAS BEEN EATING MY PORRIDGE!" said Papa Bear in a big loud voice.

When Mama Bear sat down at the kitchen table, she found a 🥄 in her 🥣 , too. "Somebody has been eating *my* porridge!" said Mama Bear in a medium-sized voice.

When Baby Bear sat down at the kitchen table, he also found a 🥄 in his 🥣 . "Somebody has been eating *my* porridge—and ate it all up!" said Baby Bear in a wee little voice.

Next Papa Bear saw that his 🪑 had been moved. "SOMEBODY HAS BEEN SITTING IN MY CHAIR!" said Papa Bear in a big loud voice.

Then Mama Bear saw that the cushion on her 🪑 was rumpled. "Somebody has been sitting in *my* chair!" said Mama Bear in a medium-sized voice.

Then Baby Bear saw that his was all in pieces. "Somebody has been sitting in *my* chair—and broke it!" cried Baby Bear in a wee little voice.

After that the bears walked up the to their bedroom. First, Papa Bear found that the pillow on his was crooked. "SOMEBODY HAS BEEN LYING ON MY BED!" said Papa Bear in a big loud voice.

Then Mama Bear found that the blanket on her was crumpled. "Somebody has been lying on *my* bed," said Mama Bear in a medium-sized voice.

Then Baby Bear saw fast asleep. "Somebody has been lying in *my* bed—and here she is!" cried Baby Bear in his wee little voice.

The voices of the woke . When she saw the bears looking at her, she jumped out of and ran down the . Then she raced out of the and through the , all the way home to her mother.

15

The Teddy Bears' Picnic

Words by
Jimmy Kennedy

Music by
John W. Bratton

cont.

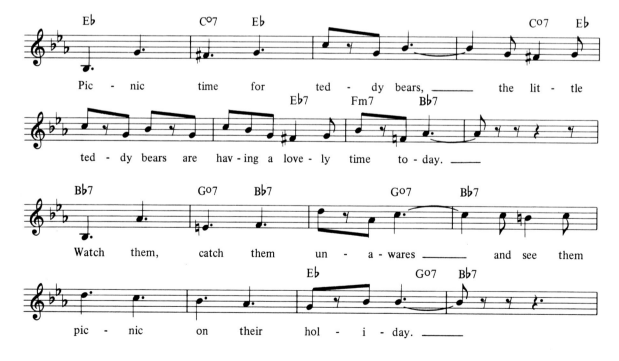

Pic - nic time for ted - dy bears, _____ the lit - tle

ted - dy bears are hav - ing a love - ly time to - day. _____

Watch them, catch them un - a - wares _____ and see them

pic - nic on their hol - i - day. _____

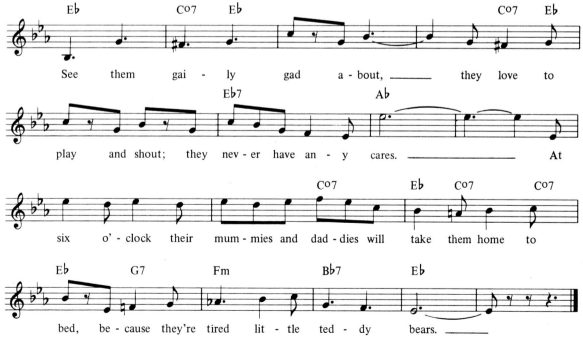

See them gai - ly gad a - bout, _____ they love to play and shout; they nev - er have an - y cares. _____ At six o' - clock their mum - mies and dad - dies will take them home to bed, be - cause they're tired lit - tle ted - dy bears. _____

The Bear

A bear got loose from the city Zoo,
He came up the street and said,
      "How do you do?"
I shook his paw and said with a smile,
"I'm fine—please stay and play awhile."

Said the big fuzzy bear,
Without ruffling a hair,
      "I'd like some bread,
      And I'd like some honey;
      But the trouble is,
      I have no money."

So I bought a honey sandwich fat,
And he gobbled it down just like that.
Then he turned so quickly and said,
Back to the Zoo I must surely fly.
      I want to go home, I do,
      I'm homesick for the Zoo.

I looked around—
      there was nothing there;
Up in thin air
      had vanished that bear!

Lois Lenski

20

A Cheerful Old Bear
at the Zoo

A cheerful old bear at the Zoo
Could always find something to do.
When it bored him, you know,
To walk to and fro,
He reversed it, and walked fro and to.

Anonymous

The Forgetful Bears

by Lawrence Weinberg

One spring morning Mrs. Forgetful woke up and went to the window. "What a beautiful day," she said. "Wake up everyone! Let's go to the country and have a picnic."

"Hooray!" shouted Sally and Tommy Forgetful. "We'll make the lemonade."

They ran to the kitchen, and squeezed lots of lemons. They added sugar. They added water. Soon the lemonade was ready. But they forgot about the picnic and drank it all themselves.

23

"I'll wake up Grandpa," said Mr. Forgetful. But he forgot where Grandpa's room was and walked into a closet. There on the shelf was his bowler hat. "Just what I'm looking for!" he said, and put it on. Then he closed the door behind him and forgot to come out.

Soon Mrs. Forgetful was ready to leave. "All right, everybody," she called. "Let's go!" But she forgot where the front door was. Instead she opened the door to the closet.

"Ah, there you are!" said Mr. Forgetful, who was standing inside. "Have you forgotten that we're going on a picnic?"

At last the four Forgetfuls found their way out of the house. They piled into their car and drove off.

Suddenly Mrs. Forgetful cried out, "Turn back! I forgot the food!"

Mr. Forgetful headed back for town. But he forgot what street they lived on and couldn't find the house.

Finally Mr. Forgetful suggested they look for their house on foot. They walked up one street and down another.

"There's our house," cried Tommy Forgetful. "No! Our house is red," said Sally Forgetful.

"Hmmm. I thought it was blue," said Mr. Forgetful. "Well, maybe we've moved," said Mrs. Forgetful. "I'm tired. Let's go back to the car."

But where was the car? Nobody could remember.

Tommy Forgetful had a bright idea. "Let's split up," he said. "Each bear will walk in a different direction. The first bear to find the car will honk the horn, and let the rest of us know where it is."

And so the four Forgetful Bears went on their separate ways.

Mrs. Forgetful walked down a street where there were many stores. A supermarket sign said, "Big Sale Today." She forgot about the car, and hurried inside to shop.

Sally Forgetful walked down another street where there was a park. She forgot about the car, and sat down to rest.

Tommy Forgetful came to a bus stop. He forgot about the car, and hopped on a bus.

Mr. Forgetful kept walking and walking. He forgot about the car, and walked straight out of town.

Meanwhile, Grandpa Forgetful woke up. He rubbed his eyes and got out of bed. "Where is everybody?" he shouted.

He went outside to look. There, across the street, was the family car. "What luck," said Grandpa. And he drove off to find the other Forgetfuls.

Soon he saw Sally Forgetful, asleep on a bench. "Poor child, she's tired," he said to himself. He stopped and carried Sally to the back seat of the car.

A little while later Grandpa saw Mrs. Forgetful leaving the supermarket. "Poor woman, she sure is loaded down," he said. He took some of her packages and helped her into the car.

Grandpa stopped for a light and saw Tommy Forgetful. "Poor boy, why is he riding on the bus?" Grandpa honked the horn. "Come with us, Tommy."

So Tommy hopped off the bus and slid in next to Grandpa. "Where are we going?" Tommy asked.

"It's such a nice day," Grandpa said. "How would you like to go for a picnic in the country?"

"What a wonderful idea!" said Mrs. Forgetful. "Why didn't *I* think of that?"

So they drove out into the country. Along the road they spotted Mr. Forgetful, walking *very* slowly. Grandpa stopped the car. "Poor man! You look tired. Hop in!" he said.

"Thank you," Mr. Forgetful said. "But I never accept rides from strangers."

"But we're your FAMILY!" shouted Mrs. Forgetful. "I'm your wife and this is your son and this is your daughter and this is your *father*!"

"Well, in that case," said Mr. Forgetful, "I guess I will get in the car. But don't tell me your names. I'm sure they will come to me."

So they drove to a lovely spot by the river. They made sandwiches from the groceries Mrs. Forgetful had bought. And they all had a wonderful time—which they never forgot.

The Bear
Went Over the Mountain

Brightly

to the tune of "For He's a Jolly Good Fellow"

1. The bear went o-ver the moun-tain, The bear went o-ver the moun-tain, The
2. He saw an-oth-er moun-tain, He saw an-oth-er moun-tain, He

bear went o-ver the moun-tain, And what do you think he saw?
saw an-oth-er moun-tain, And what do you think he did?

Chorus:

And what do you think he { saw? / did? }   And what do you think he { saw? / did? }

3. He climbed the other mountain,
   He climbed the other mountain,
   He climbed the other mountain,
   And what do you think he saw?

Chorus: And what do you think he saw?

Repeat verses 2 and 3 as many times as you wish.

The Bear Hunt

I played I was two polar bears
Who lived inside a cave of chairs,

And Brother was the hunter-man
Who tried to shoot us when we ran.

The tenpins made good bones to gnaw,
I held them down beneath my paw.

Of course, I had to kill him quick
Before he shot me with his stick.

So all the cave fell down, you see,
On Brother and the bones and me—

So then he said he wouldn't play—
But it was teatime, anyway!

Margaret Widdemer

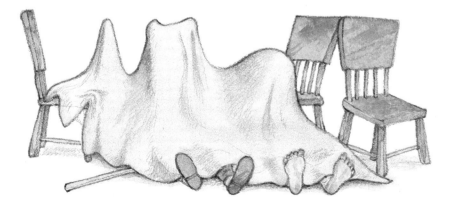

Introduction to *Little Bear*

One of the sweetest bear characters ever created is Little Bear, by Else Minarik. Little Bear is a preschooler and his patient, loving parents are the mother and father every child needs.

Nothing serious can ever harm Little Bear. Little Bear faces only the small problems that are part of a real childhood. Little Bear has a fine imagination and may believe in mermaids, but he will always go home at the end of the day to a warm supper and an early bedtime.

Else Minarik, author of the Little Bear books, was born in Denmark. She came to live in America when she was four years old. Her Little Bear stories are gentle and wise, comforting and kind.

Part of the reason Little Bear is so endearing is that he was drawn by Maurice Sendak. *Father Bear Comes Home,* the book from which the following story is taken, is the second title in the Little Bear series and was first published in 1959. At that time, Mr. Sendak had not yet written *Where the Wild Things Are* or any of his other classic children's books. Instead, he was busy concentrating on a small cub who often looks and behaves more like a child than a real child.

Little Bear's Mermaid

from FATHER BEAR COMES HOME

by Else Holmelund Minarik

pictures by Maurice Sendak

"We can picnic here," said Mother Bear.
"It is nice here, by the river."

"Let's go for a swim," said Father Bear.

Owl said,
"Little Bear swims like a fish."

"Yes," said Little Bear,
"but mermaids swim best of all.
I still wish we had a mermaid.
Maybe there is a mermaid in the river."

"I never saw one," said Cat.

"Well," said Little Bear,
"she may be shy.
She may not want us to see her.
If we could make believe we are asleep,
she might come and look at us.
Then I would jump up
and play with her."

"Oh," said Owl,
"but if she is shy,
she might jump back in the river.
Then all we could see
would be bubbles."

"Would she like us?" asked Hen.

"Of course," said Little Bear.

"She might want to play with you,"
said Mother Bear.

"I see some bubbles now,"
said Little Bear.
"And where there are bubbles,
there may be a mermaid.
I'm going in."

"If you find a mermaid,"
said Father Bear,
"ask her to picnic with us."

"Yes, do that," said Mother Bear.
"Ask her."

"I will," said Little Bear,
"because you never can tell.
She might really come back with me."

"Yes indeed," said Father Bear,
"she might really come back with you.
Because you never can tell
about mermaids.
You never can tell."

Introduction to
Why the Bear Is Stumpy-tailed

How did the world and all that's in it come to be? For generations, children and grown-ups have asked those essential questions—about the earth and sky, about man, and about animals.

"How and why stories" are folktales that provide answers to these questions. From Iceland to Africa, storytellers have told tales to explain why the sea is salty or how people first found fire. Generation after generation has heard about how the chipmunk got his stripes or why a goat can't climb a tree.

We have unearthed three "how and why" stories about bears. Since bears tend to be large, powerful animals, many stories have been created to make them seem less frightening. *Why the Bear Is Stumpy-tailed* is from Scandinavia. *Why Bear Sleeps All Winter* was first told by black people in the American South.

Why the Bear Is Stumpy-tailed

a Norse folktale

One winter day long ago, a fox was racing across the meadow with a string of stolen fish. Before he could reach the far side, he ran into a big, bushy-tailed bear.

In those days a fancy word for bear was bruin.

"Good day, Bruin," said the fox, as he tried to slink around the bear.

"Wait a moment," said the bear, hungrily eyeing the fox's string of fish. "Tell me, where in the world did you get those fish?"

"Uh—I went fishing!" lied the fox.

"But how? All the lakes are frozen, my good sir."

"Yes, yes, I know," answered the fox. "But I cut a hole in the ice and then I fished."

"I see. But you don't have a fishing pole, my friend."

"I didn't need a pole," said the fox. "I used my tail instead."

"Your tail?" said the bear. "I never heard of such a thing."

"Well, it works!" said the fox, holding up the fish. "But I must be on my way now, Bruin. Excuse me."

"Wait!" said the bear. "How long should someone keep his tail in the hole?"

"The longer the time, the more fish you will catch!" cried the fox as he ran off.

The bear lumbered to the nearest lake. Of course it was frozen. He cut a hole in the ice, turned around, and stuck his long, bushy tail in the hole.

He stayed that way until nearly sundown. By then his tail was frozen solid in the ice. When the bear tried to pull it out of the hole, the tail snapped right off.

And that is exactly why all bears have stumpy tails, to this very day.

Why Bear Sleeps All Winter

a folktale from the American South

Long ago when the world was new, the animals that lived in the woods had a problem. The problem was Bear.

Bear was a mean old thing. He was the biggest animal in the forest, and he always got his own way. When he lumbered through the trees, the smaller animals had to scatter quickly. He ate all the ripe berries off the bushes and slept in the biggest, best hollow tree in the woods.

The animals were sick and tired of being pushed around by Bear, and they decided to do something about it.

One day in autumn the animals called a meeting. "Old Man Bear is very bossy," said Owl. "We must do something."

Everyone agreed, but no one knew what to do. The animals racked their brains. The meeting stretched on day after day. Finally, Rabbit came up with an idea.

"I've got it!" said Rabbit. "Bear sleeps in a hollow tree at night, isn't that so?"

"Yes, indeed," said the animals.

"Well, why don't we stop up the tree?" said Rabbit. "That should keep him out of our hair for a while."

"Maybe he will take a long nap," said Owl. "And we will get some rest."

Everyone liked Rabbit's idea. That night, the animals
stayed up late. After Old Man Bear crawled into his hollow
tree to sleep, they went to work. They gathered sticks and
leaves and stones and stuffed up the hole in Bear's tree.

In the morning Bear woke up at the usual time, but it
was still dark inside the tree. The leaves and branches that
covered the opening were keeping out the light. Bear rolled
over, saying, "Sun's not up yet," and went right back to sleep.

Old Man Bear slept on and on in his safe, snug den. He
slept so long he slept through the winter. At last, little green
leaves sprouted on the trees. It was spring. The other animals
began to wonder why Bear hadn't woken up yet.

"Do you think he's dead?" the animals asked each other.
"Isn't he going to wake up at all?"

Finally curiosity got the best of them. They pulled away the leaves and branches and peered in at Old Man Bear.

The sunshine hit Bear in the face. He opened his eyes to little slits and blinked. Then he saw the animals staring at him. "What are you looking at?" he growled. "Haven't you ever seen a bear wake up?"

The animals scampered away and went about their business, pretending nothing had happened.

Bear yawned and stretched. He looked outside and saw the new green leaves. "The most comfortable winter I ever had!" he said to himself. "I think I'll do the same thing next year."

And Bear did the same thing the next year, and every year after that. He found himself a warm, quiet place, curled up, and slept the winter through.

The Bear and the Butterfly

The bear and the butterfly had a fight
All the day and most of the night
Till at last the bear lay waving his paws
And the butterfly lit on one of his jaws.
Oh, never struggle and never fight
With a butterfly on a moonlight night.

Margaret Wise Brown

Bear Cub's Day

Black bear cub trotted after his mother,
Tumbled and tussled in play with his brother,
Romped and roared in a wrestling match,
Snatched some lunch in a blueberry patch,
Climbed tall trees without any fear,
Fished for fish where the stream ran clear,
Curled at last in a furry heap,
Too tired for anything else but sleep.

Margaret Hillert

Grandpa Bear's Lullaby

The night is long
But fur is deep.
You will be warm
In winter sleep.

The food is gone
But dreams are sweet
And they will be
Your winter meat.

The cave is dark
But dreams are bright
And they will serve
As winter light.

Sleep, my little cubs, sleep.

Jane Yolen

Two Friends and a Bear

an Aesop fable

One day two friends were out walking in the woods. "Isn't it a fine day?" said one of the friends, whose name was Big Jack.

"Very fine," said the other, who was called Little Joe. "But isn't it dangerous in this part of the woods? I hear it's full of wild animals."

"Nothing I can't handle," said Big Jack.

Just then the two friends heard a bark in the distance.

"What was that?" asked Little Joe nervously.

"It's just a wild dog," said Big Jack. "I can take care of a wild dog with one arm tied behind my back."

"I'm glad to hear it," said Little Joe.

Just then the two friends heard a howl.

"What was *that*?" asked Little Joe, even more nervously.

"Nothing but a wolf," said Big Jack. "Don't worry. I can handle a wolf blindfolded!"

"If you say so," said Little Joe.

Just then the two friends heard a mighty roar. Little Joe jumped out of his shoes. "What was THAT?" he cried.

Before Big Jack could answer, a giant bear bounded out of the bushes. He was headed straight for them!

"Help!" cried Big Jack. The brave fellow grabbed the only nearby tree limb and hoisted himself up into the tree.

Little Joe had no idea what to do. The only thing he could think of was to throw himself flat on the ground, and that is what he did.

The bear waddled over to Little Joe, put his muzzle to Joe's ear, and sniffed. Little Joe played dead and did not move. At last the bear lost interest. He shook his large head and slouched away.

When the bear was safely out of sight, Big Jack came down out of his tree. "That was a close one, eh, Little Joe?" he said, laughing. "But tell me, what did Mister Bruin whisper in your ear?"

Little Joe beckoned to his friend. Big Jack moved closer. Then Little Joe leaned over and whispered, "The bear said, 'Never trust a friend who deserts you in a pinch.'"

With that, Little Joe headed for home, leaving Big Jack standing in the woods by himself.

Furry Bear

If I were a bear,
   And a big bear too,
I shouldn't much care
   If it froze or snew;
I shouldn't much mind
   If it snowed or friz—
I'd be all fur-lined
   With a coat like his!

For I'd have fur boots and a brown fur wrap,
And brown fur knickers and a big fur cap.
I'd have a fur muffle-ruff to cover my jaws,
And brown fur mittens on my big brown paws.
With a big brown furry-down up to my head,
I'd sleep all the winter in a big fur bed.

A. A. Milne

from
Adventures of Isabel

Isabel met an enormous bear,
Isabel, Isabel, didn't care;
The bear was hungry, the bear was ravenous,
The bear's big mouth was cruel and cavernous.
The bear said, Isabel, glad to meet you,
How do, Isabel, now I'll eat you!
Isabel, Isabel, didn't worry,
Isabel didn't scream or scurry.
She washed her hands and she straightened her hair up,
Then Isabel quietly ate the bear up.

Ogden Nash

My Teddy Bear

A teddy bear is a faithful friend.
You can pick him up at either end.
His fur is the color of breakfast toast,
And he's always there when you need him most.

Marchette Chute

The Bear and the Crow

story and illustration by Arnold Lobel

The Bear was on his way to town. He was dressed in his finest coat and vest. He was wearing his best derby hat and his shiniest shoes.

"How grand I look," said the Bear to himself. "The townsfolk will be impressed. My clothes are at the height of fashion."

"Forgive me for listening," said a Crow, who was sitting on the branch of a tree, "but I must disagree. Your clothes are *not* at the height of fashion. I have just flown in from town. I can tell you exactly how the gentlemen are dressed there."

"Do tell me!" cried the Bear. "I am so eager to wear the most proper attire!"

"This year," said the Crow, "the gentlemen are not wearing hats. They all have frying pans on their heads. They are not wearing coats and vests. They are covering themselves with bed sheets. They are not wearing shoes. They are putting paper bags on their feet."

"Oh, dear," cried the Bear, "my clothes are completely wrong!"

The Bear hurried home. He took off his coat and vest and hat and shoes. He put a frying pan on his head. He wrapped himself in a bed sheet. He stuffed his feet into large paper bags and rushed off toward the town.

When the Bear arrived on Main Street, the people giggled and smirked and pointed their fingers.

"What a ridiculous Bear!" they said.

The embarrassed Bear turned around and ran home. On the way he met the Crow again.

"Crow, you did not tell me the truth!" cried the Bear.

"I told you many things," said the Crow, as he flew out of the tree, "but never once did I tell you that I was telling the truth!"

Even though the Crow was high in the sky, the Bear could still hear the shrill sound of his cackling laughter.

When the need is strong, there are those who will believe anything.

Introduction to
Snow White and Rose Red

A fairy tale is a folktale wrapped in fantasy. It takes place in a faraway land. And often, as in the case of *Snow White and Rose Red,* the story comes from the collection of the Brothers Grimm.

The brothers, Jacob and Wilhelm, were among the first scholars in the world to take fairy tales seriously. Jacob and Wilhelm Grimm roamed their native Germany, urging people to tell them stories, especially old ones. The brothers listened carefully and wrote them down word for word.

The Grimms published their first book in 1812 and a second a few years later. Little by little, people all over the world read and translated *Grimm's Fairy Tales.*

Snow White and Rose Red is one of 211 tales collected by the Brothers Grimm. It is a magical story of two young girls, eager and kind, who are lucky enough to know a gentle, enchanted bear.

Snow White and Rose Red

a fairy tale from the Brothers Grimm

Once upon a time a poor widow lived in a lonely forest cottage. Outside the cottage were two rose trees—one with white roses, and the other with red. The woman also had two daughters—one named Snow White, and the other Rose Red.

Though the girls were very close to each other, they were quite different in nature. Snow White was quiet and gentle and liked to help her mother with the housework and read by the fire. Rose Red was brave and adventurous and liked to run in the meadows and climb tall trees.

What both sisters loved, however, was roaming through the forest together. The deer played with the girls, and the birds ate from their hands. If darkness overtook them, the sisters lay on the moss under the trees and slept until morning. Their mother never worried about them for she trusted the creatures of the forest.

But on cold winter nights, Snow White and Rose Red stayed at home. As the snow fell outside, their mother bolted the door and cooked a good supper in the kettle over the fire. After dinner she and her daughters sat by the hearth while she read stories to them.

One stormy evening, as the snow fell and the wind blew, the girls and their mother heard a knock at the door. "Who is it?" said the mother.

"Let me in, please," begged a deep voice.

Thinking a stranger was in need of shelter, the mother quickly opened the door. A great black bear stood in the shadows. He had a large head and huge paws, and when Snow White and Rose Red saw him, they screamed and hid.

"I'm sorry for disturbing you," the bear told the mother. "I only want to warm myself by your fire, for I'm half-frozen."

"You poor thing," said the mother. "Girls, come out. The bear won't harm you."

When Snow White and Rose Red crept out of their hiding place, the bear smiled at them. "Would you mind brushing the snow off my coat?" he asked.

Rose Red grabbed a broom and swept the snow off the dark, wet fur. Then she and her sister began playing with the bear. They rode on his back and danced with him around the room until finally he stretched out in front of the fire and went to sleep.

Every night thereafter, the great bear came to the cottage and played with Snow White and Rose Red until he fell asleep by the hearth.

On the first day of spring, the bear woke up in the morning and said to the sisters, "I must go away now. In the winter, the ground is frozen and the dwarfs sleep below the earth. But in the spring, when the sun warms the ground, the dwarfs come out to steal and make trouble. And I must now go into the forest and guard my treasures."

The girls were sad to see the bear leave them. They waved good-bye and wept as he disappeared into the woods.

One day, a few weeks later, when Snow White and Rose Red were in the forest collecting firewood, they saw a small creature in the distance, jumping about like a dog on a rope. When they crept closer, they discovered it was a withered old dwarf. His long white beard was caught in the crevice of a tree.

"Don't just stare like two idiots!" the dwarf shouted at them. "Help me!"

Snow White and Rose Red tugged on the dwarf's beard, but they could not untangle it from the tree. Finally Rose Red pulled a pair of sewing scissors out of her pocket and snipped off the end of the beard, freeing the dwarf.

Instead of being thankful, the little man was furious. "You stupid goose!" he shouted. "Look at what you just did! You hurt my glorious beard!"

Lying near the tree was a bag of gold. Without another word, the dwarf picked up the bag and stalked away.

Not long afterward, Snow White and Rose Red set out to catch fish for their supper. Coming to the stream, they saw a creature leaping about the bank like a giant grasshopper. As they crept closer, they realized it was the same ancient dwarf.

This time, his beard was caught in his fishing line. A big fish at the end of the line was pulling him back and forth mercilessly.

To save the dwarf, Snow White pulled out a pair of scissors and snipped off some more of his long beard.

But instead of showing gratitude, the dwarf was enraged. "You hateful girl!" he shouted. "This time my beard's completely ruined!"

On the bank of the stream was a bag of pearls. Without another word, the dwarf picked up the bag and hobbled away.

A week later, Snow White and Rose Red went to town to buy needles and thread for their mother. On their way through the woods, they heard a pitiful scream. They ran to find out what was happening and saw an enormous eagle dragging the dwarf by his beard.

"Help! Help!" shrieked the little man as the giant bird began to lift him into the air.

The girls grabbed hold of the dwarf's arms and coat. They pulled and tugged until finally the eagle let go of the little man. But instead of rewarding the two sisters, the dwarf cursed them. "You clumsy fools!" he shouted. "You tore my coat!"

Lying on the ground was a bag of precious stones. Without another word, the dwarf picked up the bag and stalked away.

On their way home, Snow White and Rose Red came upon the dwarf once again. This time he was sitting in the forest, admiring all the treasure spread out before him. The two sisters stopped and gaped at the glittering gold, the shining pearls, and the precious stones.

When the dwarf saw them, he flew into a rage. "You witches!" he shrieked. "No one is allowed to spy on me!"

57

But just as he leapt forward to strike the girls, a great black bear lumbered out from behind the trees. With one blow, he knocked the dwarf dead.

It was the same bear that had visited the girls during the winter. Turning toward the two of them, the shaggy figure suddenly shed his bearskin. And standing there instead was a handsome young man, clothed in gold.

Snow White and Rose Red cried out in astonishment.

"Don't be frightened," said the young man. "I'm the son of a king. The dwarf used his evil powers to turn me into a wild bear. Then he stole my treasures. Only his death could set me free. Until then, I had to live in the forest as a wild animal."

The handsome prince took the sisters to his castle by the sea. He asked Snow White to marry him, and his brother asked Rose Red for her hand in marriage.

The two princesses sent for their mother to come live with them. When their mother came, she brought her rose trees with her, the white and the red. The trees were planted in front of the castle. From that time on, roses were in bloom both summer and winter, and everyone lived happily ever after.

How the First Bears Came

Native American legend
retold by Carolyn Sherwin Bailey

Once upon a time, there were only Indians upon the earth, and the tribes had a Great Spirit who was their ruler. He had a little daughter, the Wind-Child.

It was thought that the Great Spirit and his daughter lived in the largest wigwam of the world. It was a mountain that stood, tall and pointed, on the edge of the sea. The winds raged about the sea coast, and no one seemed to have any power over them except the Wind-Child. They would sometimes obey her, if she came out of her father's wigwam, the mountain, and begged them to be still.

No wonder the winds obeyed the Wind-Child. Her eyes were as bright as the stars when the west wind blew the clouds away from the sky at night. She was as fleet and strong as the north wind. She could sing as sweetly as did the south wind. And her hair was as long and soft as the mists that the east wind carried.

The Wind-Child had only one fault. She was very curious about matters that did not concern her.

One day, when the winter was almost over, there was a gale at sea. The surf rolled up and beat against the Great Spirit's mountain. The wind was so strong that the mountain shook. It seemed as if it would topple over. The Great Spirit spoke to his daughter.

"Go out to the lodge of the cave, at the base of the mountain," he said, "and reach out your arm and ask the wind to cease. But do not go beyond the cave, for the storm rages and it is not safe for you to go any farther."

So the Wind-Child did as her father had asked her. She stood at the edge of the cave. She stretched out her arm and the wind quieted. Then the Wind-Child forgot to obey her father. The sun came out, and she saw many bright shells lying on the sand. The waves had washed them up during the storm. She left the mountain, and ran along the beach gathering shells.

As soon as the Wind-Child had picked up one shell, she dropped it to go on farther in search of one that was larger. On and on she went, always looking for a shell that was brighter. She suddenly found that she had gone a long way from home. She could not see the wigwam. She found herself, where the magic trail of the shells had led her, in a deep, dark forest. It was a frightful place, and the trees shut the Wind-Child in on all sides.

The forest was settled by a strange race of grizzly people. They were dark, rough in their ways, and wore shaggy fur clothing. Their wigwams were made of the trunks of trees.

They had great fires in the open places of the woods about which they sat. They seemed glad to see the Wind-Child. The mothers crowded around her, and the children brought her nuts. They gave her a fur cloak and one of the best wigwams in which to live. When the Wind-Child begged to go home to her father, these grizzly people of the forest gave her sweets to eat. They let her taste of the thick, sweet maple syrup that they cooked in their kettles. They gave her wild honey that the bees had left the season before in the hollow trees. After eating these, the Wind-Child forgot all about her home, and lived with and learned the ways of these forest people. Years and years passed and she was still among them, grown as wild and savage as they themselves were.

The Great Spirit looked for his daughter season after season all over the earth, and still he could not find her. His mountain was deserted. His voice could be heard calling her in every wind that blew. Great drought and famine came upon the land because he neglected the earth. It was a time of great suffering. But one day he came upon the grizzly people. They were moving their camp from one part of the forest to another. In their midst was the Wind-Child, looking almost like one of them. She knew her father, though, and ran to him, begging to go home with him. He took her in his arms, but he turned in anger toward her captors.

As the Great Spirit gazed in anger upon the grizzly people, they drew their fur cloaks over their heads. They dropped down to the ground at his feet to beg for mercy. The Great Spirit left the forest. As he did so these wild people of the woods found that they could not rise to their feet again. They were not able to draw their fur cloaks from their heads. They went about on all fours, covered from head to foot with shaggy fur. They could not speak, but could only growl.

63

They were the first bears, and there have been bears ever since in place of the strange savages who captured the Wind-Child.

The Great Spirit took the Wind-Child to the top of the mountain, and they lived there always. On her return the rain fell and the sun shone, and there was plenty in the earth again. But the bear tribe prowled the earth, hunted by the Indians, because of the Wind-Child's curiosity.

Kunikdjuaq

a bear story of the Inuit
retold by Maria Leach

Way north in Alaska there was a little village of the Eskimo people who call themselves Inuit. (*Inuit* means men.) There were only a few little houses in the village strung along the cold waters of the Arctic shore, and in one of them lived a lonely old woman. She had no strong young son of her own to go hunting and fishing for her or bring home meat and fish.

One day she found a little white polar bear cub all alone on the ice. Someone must have killed his mother, she thought, so she took him home.

65

The cub's name was Kunikdjuaq. The old woman fed him as best she could. She gave him half her own food—and that was only what she got from the neighbors. For this is the custom among the Inuit when someone has made a good catch—to share the food with the village. But the cub grew tall and smart, and in the spring he soon learned to hunt salmon and seal himself, which he brought home to the old woman. The children of the village loved him. They used to play with him and roll and tumble him in the snow like a little white ball.

Soon the old woman had plenty to eat. She fed the cub on great slices of blubber from the fat seals he caught, and they were very happy together.

The old woman was very proud. Now she too could run to the door and call "Come!" to the people of the village, whenever Kunikdjuaq brought home a specially fine seal or salmon.

Kunikdjuaq was a wonderful hunter. He was far more skillful and successful than the grown men of the village. They began to be envious. Their envy grew so big that finally they decided to kill the young bear. The children heard the people talking and ran and told the old woman.

The old woman went to all the houses, one by one, and begged them not to kill her beautiful cub. "Do not kill my son," she said. She begged them to kill her instead. But the people would not listen. They were determined to get rid of Kunikdjuaq. They said he was fat and would make a fine feast for the whole village.

The old woman ran home quickly then and told the young bear that his life was in danger. "Run away," she said. "Run away and don't come back." Then because her heart was breaking, she begged him not to go too far—not so far that she could not find him once in a while, she said.

So Kunikdjuaq went away. The old woman grieved bitterly to see him go. And so did the children of the village.

After a while the old woman again had no food, so she went far out on the sea ice looking for her son. She always called him "my son." Soon she saw him and called his name. He heard her and ran to meet her.

She patted him and looked him over to see if he had been
hurt in any fights. But the young bear was fat and strong and
sleek and white and glossy. Then the old woman told him she
needed food.

Off went Kunikdjuaq and came back in a short time
with meat and fish. The old woman cut it up in slices with
her knife and gave him many big pieces of the blubber before
she carried the meat home.

This went on for many years. And today the Inuit still
tell this "story of unbroken love" between the old woman and
her bear.

The Bear and the Squirrels

by C. P. Cranch

There was an old Bear that lived near a wood
   (His name it was Growly, Growly),
   Where two little Squirrels gathered their food,
With a ramble, scramble, chittery tit!
   O, a terrible fellow was Growly!

The two little Squirrels they lived in a tree,
   Growly, Growly, Growly!
They were so merry, and happy, and free,
With a ramble, scramble, chittery tit!
   "Don't come near me," says Growly.

The Squirrels were rather afraid of the Bear,
   Growly, Growly, Growly,
With his claws, and his teeth, and his shaggy hair;
For their ramble, scramble, chittery tit,
   Made too much noise for Growly.

So whenever the Bear came into the wood,
   Growly, Growly, Growly!
The Squirrels ran, and dropped their food,
With a ramble, scramble, chittery tit!
   "Those nuts are all mine," says Growly.

70

One day old Bruin lay down in the shade,
    Growly, Growly, Growly,
Under the tree where the Squirrels played,
With a ramble, scramble, chittery tit!
    "I'll just take a nap," says Growly.

Old Bruin then began to snore,
    Growly, Growly, Growly;
Said the Squirrels, "We'd rather hear that than a roar;
With a ramble, scramble, chittery tit!
    We'll wake you up, old Growly!"

So, plump on his nose a nut they dropped,
    Growly, Growly, Growly!
When all of a sudden the snoring stopped,
With a ramble, scramble, chittery tit!
    "Plague take the flies!" says Growly.

So he turned him round to sleep again,
    Growly, Growly, Growly,
When down came the nuts like a patter of rain,
With a ramble, scramble, chittery tit!
    "It's hailing!" says Sir Growly.

"No matter," says Bruin, "I'll have my nap!"
    Growly, Growly, Growly;
So he slept again, when tap, tap, tap,
With a ramble, scramble, chittery tit,
    They pelted him well, old Growly.

Then up he sprang and looked all around,
    Growly, Growly, Growly;
But nothing he saw, and he heard no sound
But a ramble, scramble, chittery tit,
    "Why, what can it be?" says Growly.

At last he looked up into the tree,
  Growly, Growly, Growly!
And there the little rogues saw he,
With a ramble, scramble, chittery tit!
  "Why, what's the matter, old Growly?"

"You often have made the poor Squirrels run,
  Growly, Growly, Growly!
So now we thought *we* would have some fun,
With a ramble, scramble, chittery tit!"
  "It served me right," says Growly.

And so the old fellow he saw the joke,
  Growly, Growly, Growly!
And began to laugh till they thought he'd choke
With a ramble, scramble, Ha, ha, ha!
  "What a capital joke!" says Growly.

Sir Bruin then grew gentle and mild,
  Growly, Growly, Growly!
And played with the squirrels like a child
With a ramble, scramble, chittery tit,
  And lost the name of Growly.

Introduction to
The Bear on the Motorcycle

The Bear on the Motorcycle is the story of a circus bear. For centuries people have loved watching trained bears perform. In Europe in the Middle Ages, street musicians such as the organ grinder you will meet in *The Dancing Bear* often brought bears with them to dance to the music of the small hand organs. After the bear's performance, the musician would pass the hat for money.

Like the bear in Reiner Zimnik's story, bears *can* learn to ride motorcycles. Bears can also play musical instruments, do handstands, roller skate, or hold a parasol—while balancing on top of a ball!

Even when they are trained, however, bears have a wildness that never disappears completely. Lions and tigers are in fact easier to handle than bears. One reason is that a trainer can look at the expression on the face of a big cat and know how it is feeling. This is not true with bears. A trainer cannot always sense what mood a bear is in.

Performing bears look lovable, and we love to watch them. A large bear driving a little motorcycle or lumbering along in a pom-pom hat and a pink ballet skirt is a sweet and silly sight indeed.

The Bear
on the Motorcycle

by Reiner Zimnik
translated from the German by Cornelius Schaeffer

Once upon a time there was a fat brown bear. He lived in the Bumblefus circus, a contented, friendly animal. He spent the days lying behind the bars of his cage. When the weather was fine he was pleased, and he let the sun warm his rough fur; and when it rained he was pleased, too, and watched the raindrops as they fell beyond the bars. And when somebody said to him, "How are you, fat brown bear?" he would rumble in a deep voice: "Hmm. . . . Just no excitement, please. Just quiet, please."

In the evenings, when the big circus tent was filled with people, his keeper would lead him into the great arena, and another circus man would bring out a red motorcycle and start the motor. Then the fat brown bear would sit down on the motorcycle, step on the gas, and ride the motorcycle around in thirteen circles. Every single evening, and on Sunday afternoons, too.

He was the only bear in all the world who could ride a motorcycle; and every evening the people would clap their hands and shout: "Hurray for the fat brown bear, hurray, hurray." And Sunday afternoons, too.

But one day, just as he was going around for the tenth time, a little boy called out, "The bear's stupid; the bear's stupid—all he can do is go around in circles." And even though his mother and his four aunts told him, "Be quiet, it may be nothing special for a person to ride a motorcycle, but for a bear it's a fantastic achievement," the boy kept shouting, "The bear's stupid! The bear's stupid!" And at the end he shouted one more time, very loud, "Circles, just circles."

The bear understood every word, and he was very angry. On the outside nothing showed; but on the inside, underneath his thick fur, he was very excited.

"They think I'm stupid," he growled to himself. "Those children think I'm stupid. Just because I keep riding around in circles, they think I'm stupid. Hmm, I'll show them. I'll show them I'm not stupid."

77

The next day, when he had finished his thirteenth round, he didn't get off the motorcycle. And when the keeper came to take it away, he honked loudly on the horn three times and then, just as fast as he could go, he rode straight out of the circus tent. Even when he was outside the tent, he didn't stop; he rode straight past his cage, out of the circus gate, and still going as fast as he could go, he rode straight into town.

He rode straight down the main street. As he crossed the main intersection, the traffic policeman's whistle fell out of his mouth, he was so surprised. He had seen fire engines and racing cars and trucks with eight wheels, but never a bear on a red motorcycle.

"Unbelievable," he muttered to himself. "Simply unbelievable."

He hardly recovered when two minutes later, there, running along, came the keeper and the director of the circus and a lot of other people from the circus. Even from far away he could hear them shouting, "Have you seen a bear? A bear on a red motorcycle? Which way did he go?"

"Straight ahead," the policeman said quickly, showing them the way.

So the keeper and the director and the other people from the circus kept running, straight ahead.

And the traffic policeman muttered again, "Unbelievable. Really unbelievable."

In the meantime, the fat brown bear was riding his motorcycle up and down through the town; down main streets and up side streets, sometimes turning right at a corner, sometimes turning left, doing just as he pleased.

Everywhere he went people leaned out of windows, their mouths wide open for the wonder of it all. Those who had no windows on the street rushed into their hallways shouting, "What is it? What's all the noise about?"

79

And the others answered, "Come here quick! Look at that! A fat brown bear is riding a red motorcycle up and down the streets. Oh, look now! All those circus people are running after him, and they can't catch him. Oh, it's funny; oh, it's so funny!"

Some people on the sidewalks stopped and clapped their hands. Other were scared and ran into doorways or hid behind cars.

But after a while the red motorcycle ran slower and slower. There was beginning to be no more gas in the tank. Finally, the motor went *put put put* . . . and stopped. The fat brown bear got off, leaned the motorcycle against a lamppost, and sat down at the edge of the sidewalk to wait.

When the keeper and the director and all the other people from the circus came running up, panting and puffing, he waved at them gaily with his bear-paw and growled: "Hmm. . . . Just no excitement, please. Just quiet, please."

He was, you see, a friendly, contented animal, and he didn't really want to run away. He just wanted to show people that he wasn't stupid and that he really could do something besides just ride around in circles under a big tent.

So the circus people calmed down, and they mopped their brows, and then they all went to the inn down the street and ordered root beer because they were thirsty from all that running.

The keeper put the fat brown bear on a leash and, pushing the motorcycle, led the fat brown bear back to the circus.

And from that day on nobody ever shouted, "The bear is stupid!" And the bear, himself, no longer went around in circles. Now every evening he rode figure-eights and zigzags; and when he was in an especially good mood, he rode with no hands and on one wheel.

And when the performance was at an end and he was trotting his way back to his cage, he'd turn around one last time, squint up to the top rows where the children sat and, one paw raised to his bear-brow, he'd rumble, "Just let's see *you* do that!"

The Dancing Bear

by Albert Bigelow Paine

Oh, it's fiddle-de-dum and fiddle-de-dee,
The dancing bear ran away with me;
For the organ-grinder he came to town
With a jolly old bear in a coat of brown.
And the funny old chap joined hands with me,
While I cut a caper and so did he.
Then 'twas fiddle-de-dum and fiddle-de-dee,
I looked at him, and he winked at me,
And I whispered a word in his shaggy ear,
And I said, "I will go with you, my dear."

Then the dancing bear he smiled and said,
Well, he didn't say much, but he nodded his head,
As the organ-grinder began to play
"Over the hills and far away."
With a fiddle-de-dum and a fiddle-de-dee;
Oh, I looked at him and he winked at me,
And my heart was light and the day was fair,
And away I went with the dancing bear.

83

Oh, 'tis fiddle-de-dum and fiddle-de-dee,
The dancing bear came back with me;
For the sugar-plum trees were stripped and bare,
And we couldn't find cookies anywhere.
And the solemn old fellow he sighed and said,
Well, he didn't say much, but he shook his head,
While I looked at him and he blinked at me
Till I shed a tear and so did he;
And both of us thought of our supper that lay
Over the hills and far away.
Then the dancing bear he took my hand,
And we hurried away through the twilight land;
And 'twas fiddle-de-dum and fiddle-de-dee
When the dancing bear came back with me.

In Which We Are Introduced to

Winnie-the-Pooh and Some Bees, and the Stories Begin

from WINNIE-THE-POOH

by A. A. Milne

decorations by Ernest H. Shepard

Once upon a time, a very long time ago now, about last Friday, Winnie-the-Pooh lived in a forest all by himself under the name of Sanders.

("What does 'under the name' mean?" asked Christopher Robin.
"It means he had the name over the door in gold letters, and lived under it."
"Winnie-the-Pooh wasn't quite sure," said Christopher Robin.
"Now I am," said a growly voice.
"Then I will go on," said I.)

One day when he was out walking, he came to an open place in the middle of the forest, and in the middle of this place was a large oak-tree, and, from the top of the tree, there came a loud buzzing-noise.

Winnie-the-Pooh sat down at the foot of the tree, put his head between his paws and began to think.

First of all he said to himself: "That buzzing-noise means something. You don't get a buzzing-noise like that, just buzzing and buzzing, without it meaning something. If there's a buzzing-noise, somebody's making a buzzing-noise, and the only reason for making a buzzing-noise that *I* know of is because you're a bee."

Then he thought another long time, and said: "And the only reason for being a bee that I know of is making honey."

And then he got up, and said: "And the only reason for making honey is so as *I* can eat it." So he began to climb the tree.

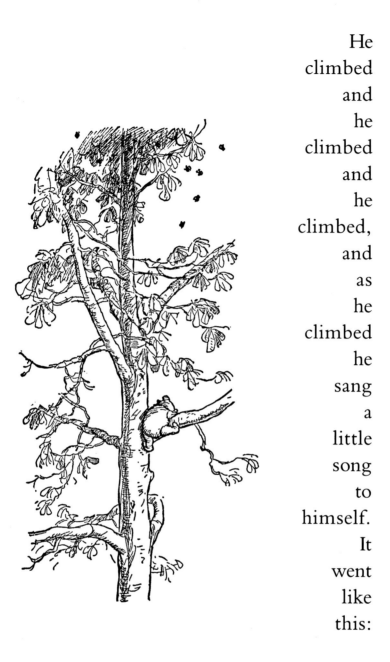

He
climbed
and
he
climbed
and
he
climbed,
and
as
he
climbed
he
sang
a
little
song
to
himself.
It
went
like
this:

Isn't it funny
How a bear likes honey?
Buzz! Buzz! Buzz!
I wonder why he does?

Then he climbed a little further...and a little further
... and then just a little further. By that time he had thought
of another song.

88

It's a very funny thought that, if Bears were Bees,
They'd build their nests at the *bottom* of trees.
And that being so (if the Bees were Bears),
We shouldn't have to climb up all these stairs.

He was getting rather tired by this time, so that is why
he sang a Complaining Song. He was nearly there now, and if
he just stood on that branch...

Crack!

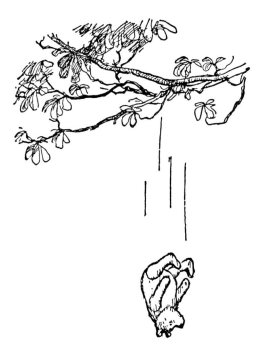

"Oh, help!" said Pooh, as he dropped ten feet on the
branch below him.

"If only I hadn't—" he said, as he bounced twenty feet
on to the next branch.

"You see, what I *meant* to do," he explained, as he turned
head-over-heels, and crashed on to another branch thirty feet
below, "what I *meant* to do—"

"Of course, it *was* rather—" he admitted, as he slithered
very quickly through the next six branches.

"It all comes, I suppose," he decided, as he said good-bye to the last branch, spun round three times, and flew gracefully into a gorse-bush, "it all comes of *liking* honey so much. Oh, help!"

He crawled out of the gorse-bush, brushed the prickles from his nose, and began to think again. And the first person he thought of was Christopher Robin.

("Was that me?" said Christopher Robin in an awed voice, hardly daring to believe it.

"That was you."

Christopher Robin said nothing, but his eyes got larger and larger, and his face got pinker and pinker.)

So Winnie-the-Pooh went round to his friend Christopher Robin, who lived behind a green door in another part of the forest.

"Good morning, Christopher Robin," he said.

"Good morning, Winnie-*ther*-Pooh," said you.

"I wonder if you've got such a thing as a balloon about you?"

"A balloon?"

"Yes, I just said to myself coming along: 'I wonder if Christopher Robin has such a thing as a balloon about him?' I just said it to myself, thinking of balloons, and wondering."

"What do you want a balloon for?" you said.

Winnie-the-Pooh looked round to see that nobody was listening, put his paw to his mouth, and said in a deep whisper: "*Honey!*"

"But you don't get honey with balloons!"

"*I* do," said Pooh.

Well, it just happened that you had been to a party the day before at the house of your friend Piglet, and you had balloons at the party. You had a big green balloon; and one of Rabbit's relations had had a big blue one, and had left it behind, being really too young to go to a party at all; and so you had brought the green one *and* the blue one home with you.

"Which one would you like?" you asked Pooh.

He put his head between his paws and thought very carefully.

"It's like this," he said. "When you go after honey with a balloon, the great thing is not to let the bees know you're coming. Now, if you have a green balloon, they might think you were only part of the tree, and not notice you, and if you have a blue balloon, they might think you were only part of the sky, and not notice you, and the question is: Which is most likely?"

"Wouldn't they notice *you* underneath the balloon?" you asked.

"They might or they might not," said Winnie-the-Pooh. "You never can tell with bees." He thought for a moment and said: "I shall try to look like a small black cloud. That will deceive them."

"Then you had better have the blue balloon," you said; and so it was decided.

Well, you both went out with the blue balloon, and you took your gun with you, just in case, as you always did, and Winnie-the-Pooh went to a very muddy place that he knew of, and rolled and rolled and rolled until he was black all over; and then, when the balloon was blown up as big as big, and you and Pooh were both holding on to the string, you let go suddenly, and Pooh Bear floated gracefully up into the sky, and stayed there—level with the top of the tree and about twenty feet away from it.

"Hooray!" you shouted.

"Isn't that fine?" shouted Winnie-the-Pooh down to you. "What do I look like?"

"You look like a Bear holding on to a balloon," you said.

"Not," said Pooh anxiously, "—not like a small black cloud in a blue sky?"

"Not very much."

"Ah, well, perhaps from up here it looks different. And, as I say, you never can tell with bees."

There was no wind to blow him nearer to the tree, so there he stayed. He could see the honey, he could smell the honey, but he couldn't quite reach the honey.

After a little while he called down to you.

"Christopher Robin!" he said in a loud whisper.

"Hallo!"

"I think the bees *suspect* something!"

"What sort of thing?"

"I don't know. But something tells me that they're *suspicious!*"

"Perhaps they think that you're after their honey."

"It may be that. You never can tell with bees."

There was another little silence, and then he called down to you again.

"Christopher Robin!"

"Yes?"

"Have you an umbrella in your house?"

"I think so."

"I wish you would bring it out here, and walk up and down with it, and look up at me every now and then, and say 'Tut-tut, it looks like rain.' I think, if you did that, it would help the deception which we are practising on these bees."

Well, you laughed to yourself, "Silly old Bear!" but you didn't say it aloud because you were so fond of him, and you went home for your umbrella.

"Oh, there you are!" called down Winnie-the-Pooh, as soon as you got back to the tree. "I was beginning to get anxious. I have discovered that the bees are now definitely Suspicious."

"Shall I put my umbrella up?" you said.

"Yes, but wait a moment. We must be practical. The important bee to deceive is the Queen Bee. Can you see which is the Queen Bee from down there?"

"No."

"A pity. Well, now, if you walk up and down with your umbrella, saying, 'Tut-tut, it looks like rain,' I shall do what I can by singing a little Cloud Song, such as a cloud might sing. . . .Go!"

So, while you walked up and down and wondered if it would rain, Winnie-the-Pooh sang this song:

How sweet to be a Cloud
    Floating in the Blue!
Every little Cloud
Always sings aloud.

"How sweet to be a Cloud
    Floating in the Blue!"
It makes him very proud
To be a little cloud.

The bees were still buzzing as suspiciously as ever. Some of them, indeed, left their nest and flew all around the cloud as it began the second verse of this song, and one bee sat down on the nose of the cloud for a moment, and then got up again.

"Christopher—*ow!*—Robin," called out the cloud.

"Yes?"

"I have just been thinking, and I have come to a very important decision. *These are the wrong sort of bees.*"

"Are they?"

"Quite the wrong sort. So I should think they would make the wrong sort of honey, shouldn't you?"

"Would they?"

"Yes. So I think I shall come down."

"How?" asked you.

Winnie-the-Pooh hadn't thought about this. If he let go of the string, he would fall—*bump*—and he didn't like the idea of that. So he thought for a long time, and then he said:

"Christopher Robin, you must shoot the balloon with your gun. Have you got your gun?"

"Of course I have," you said. "But if I do that, it will spoil the balloon," you said.

"But if you *don't*," said Pooh, "I shall have to let go, and that would spoil *me*."

When you put it like this, you saw how it was, and you aimed very carefully at the balloon, and fired.

"*Ow!*" said Pooh.

"Did I miss?" you asked.

"You didn't exactly *miss*," said Pooh, "but you missed the *balloon*."

"I'm so sorry," you said, and you fired again, and this time you hit the balloon, and the air came slowly out, and Winnie-the-Pooh floated down to the ground.

But his arms were so stiff from holding on to the string of the balloon all that time that they stayed up straight in the air for more than a week, and whenever a fly came and settled on his nose he had to blow it off. And I think—but I am not sure—that *that* is why he was always called Pooh.

Good Night, Good Night

The dark is dreaming.
Day is done.
Good night, good night
To everyone.

Good night to the birds,
And the fish in the sea,
Good night to the bears
And good night to me.

Dennis Lee

96